COME VISIT THE TEENY TINY TOWN OF TASTE

by

Orietta Gianjorio

Illustrated by Nathalie Fabri

Copyright© 2013 Orietta Gianjorio
All rights reserved.
ISBN-13:978-1494445768
ISBN-10:149444576X
First Edition: January 2014

CONTENTS

INTRODUCTION

When I moved to the United States a few years ago, I can't deny it, I felt lonely. I missed my country. Then *Coratina* came into my life. She reminded me of the importance of my Italian family but also of the one I found here.

Now, after one more year in this beautiful country, five little friends have again come to my rescue. Sweetie, Salty, Sour, Bitter, and Umami have appeared in my life to teach me a couple of important lessons.

The first lesson is acceptance, the ability to be open and learn from those who are different from us. Every day, I learn something new from my devoted American husband, but only if I keep my heart and my mind open.

The second lesson is moderation. In this fast paced society, where large portions of fast food are available at any time, it is a daily struggle to cook at home, sit leisurely around the table and find time to carefully savor our food, using sight, smell and taste.

If my first children's book, *Coratina*, is a story of self-discovery, *Come Visit the Teeny Tiny Town of Taste* is a story of acceptance and moderation. And while children are having fun with my adorable characters, I hope they will learn to *taste* their food. Maybe Sweetie, Salty, Sour, Bitter, and Umami, as well as all the charming little taste buds, will spark their interest enough to remember to call upon them when they eat.

I hope that with this book and a better understanding of our ability to taste, the next generation will be able to enjoy food in moderation and to naturally make better food choices.

For these reasons, I dedicate this book to the next generation, hoping they will eat healthy food with joy and passion, tasting every bite of it. And hoping that they will learn how to live together in harmony, by respecting each other, without antagonism. Because in this world we are all one big family and, as different as we are, during our short stay, we can make the world a fun place to visit, just like *The Teeny Tiny Town of Taste*.

COME VISIT the TEENY TINY TOWN OF TASTE and discover how much FUN you can have every day.

The TOWN OF TASTE is certainly a TEENY TINY TOWN, but it is a HAPPY one! Each day is different. Each day is special. ANYTHING can happen at ANY TIME.

The TEENY TINY TOWN OF TASTE is so TEENY TINY that it can only fit four residents: Sweetie, SALTY, Sour, and Bitter. These four residents have very DIfferENT PErsonAli+iES, but they have lived together forever, and they DEFINITELY make the TEENY TINY TOWN OF TASTE a FUN place to visit.

The TEENY TINY TOWN OF TASTE is located in the state of TONGUE.
TONGUE has THOUSANDS of citizens, and they all call each other
"Bud".

Let's get closer and meet the Buds. They are nice and friendly. They
are outgoing and sociable. They are spunky, and they definitely like to
have FUN!

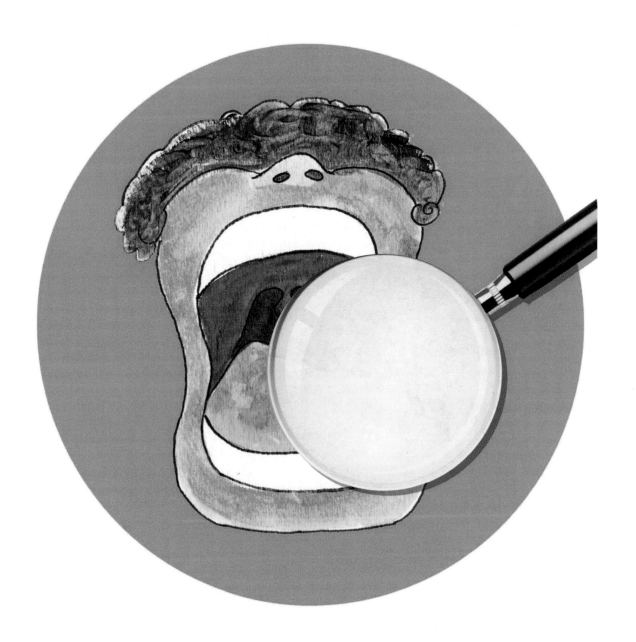

All the Buds are VERY active, and they like to stay in the state of TONGUE only for a VERY short time. But TONGUE is always busy and, as soon as one Bud leaves, another one arrives.

Always looking for fun, the Buds know well that they can find it in the TEENY TINY TOWN OF TASTE. So, several times a day, they jump on their BUS and they take field trip, after field trip, after field trip to the TEENY TINY TOWN OF TASTE. There, each day is different. Each day is special. ANYTHING can happen at ANY TIME.

On their **BUS**, the **Buds** **sing** and **dANCE** because they

know well how **FUN** it is to visit the **TEENY TINY TOWN OF TASTE**.

"We are **Buds** and we like to have **FUN**. We take *trips* to the

state of TONGUE.

We STOP here and we STOP there, the TOWN OF **TASTE** is like a

Fair".

One day, on a regular field trip, while the Buds are travelling and singing, singing and dancing, as always they decide to STOP at the home of Sweetie.

Sweetie is a popular girl, the most popular resident of the TEENY TINY TOWN OF TASTE. She is so popular that She never spends a moment alone.

"Every Bud asks for me. Every Bud wants to spend time with me! I'm so Likable! I'm so Sweet! I'm a Cheerleader, and I like to dance. I dance, I cheer, I Tumble, and I flip all the time. I never rest, I never STOP. I never STOP, I never rest... until I drop".

Sweetie really likes to have visitors, so She has built a **Big Castle**, a Sugary one. Sweetie's **Big Castle** has a roof made of gingerbread, **walls** of **milk chocolate bars**, and floors of chocolate chip and peanut butter COOKIES. The ceiling is made of Vanilla ice-cream and the WINDOWS of CLEAR CANDY LOLLIPOP. All the doors are made of cheesecake, and all the knObs of Marshmallows. The furniture is built with sugar candies and fudge brownies.

The Buds love Sweetie's Big Castle. On each trip they take, they can't wait to visit Her. As soon as they enter, they take a mouthFUL of the gingerbread roof and a huge BITE of the milk chocolate walls. Then, they gobble on the chocolate chip and peanut butter cookies floors, they gulp a giant scoop of the Vanilla ice-cream ceiling, and they suck for a very long time on the LOLLIPOP WINDOWS. To follow, they CHOMP on a GIGANTIC taste of the cheesecake doors, and they Wolf down all of the Marshmallows knobs. To finish, they swallow one by one all the sugar candies and fudge brownies furniture.

The more the Bugs bite, gobble, gulp, suck, and CHOMP Sweetie's Big Castle, the more they want to bite, gobble, gulp, suck, and CHOMP... but the more the Bugs bite, gobble, gulp, suck, and CHOMP the more they Run, Jump, dANCE, Spin, and Roll Around.

Until, all of a sudden, the Bugs STOP! They no longer Run, Jump, dANCE, Spin, and Roll Around. They have no more ENERGY. They are TIRED, Weary, exhausted, drained, Sleepy, and drowsy. They lie on the chocolate chip and peanut butter cOOKIES crumbs, and they are DONE!

Sweetie looks at the Buds kindly and thinks:

"Like all the other *field trips*, the Buds couldn't *pace* themselves. They always **bite**, *gobble*, **gULP**, *suck*, and **CHOMP too much** of my Sweet **Big Castle**".

Then, Sweetie talks to the Buds:

"Pretty little Buds why can't you learn? Mine is a Sweet **Castle**, I understand your lOve, Sweethearts. But just take a little **bite**, take a small **CHOMP**.

Why do you NEVER learn? Moderation is the *key*. Not **too much**, not too little".

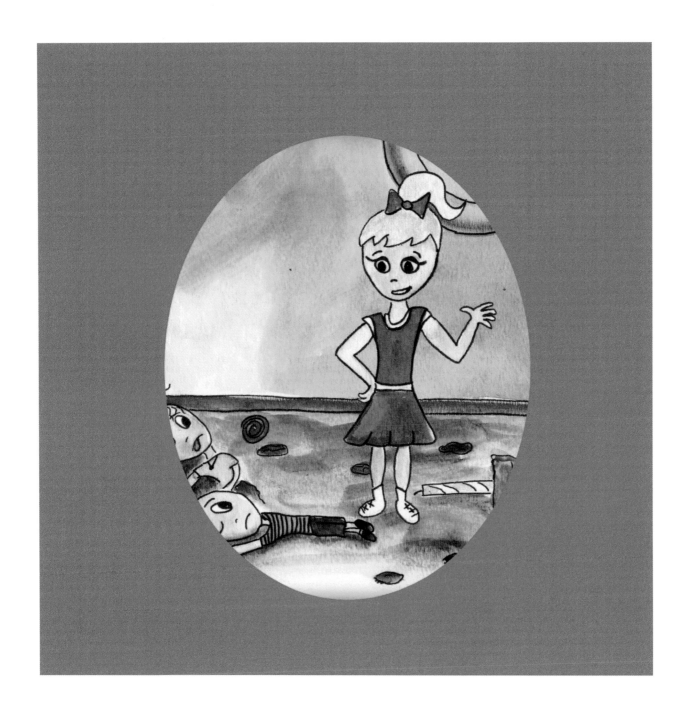

While Sweetie is talking, the Buds slowly GET UP, slowly dust off some of the chocolate chip and peanut butter COOKIE crumbs and slowly get ready to leave.

On their BUS, the Buds try to sing and dance. They know how FUN it is to visit the TEENY TINY TOWN OF TASTE, but they are so TIRED.

"We are Buds and we like to have FUN. We take trips to the

STATE of TONGUE.

We STOP here and we STOP there, the TOWN OF TASTE is like a

Fair".

Traveling and *slowly* singing, singing and *slowly* dancing, as always the Buds decide to STOP at the home of SALTY.

SALTY is an Exciting guy, the most Exciting resident of the TEENY TINY TOWN OF TASTE. HE is so Exciting that HE rarely spends a moment alone.

"Every Bud likes me. Every Bud enjoys me. I'm so witty. I'm so pungent. I'm a Skateboarder, and I like to flip. I Skate, I flip, and I *grab my* Skateboard *in the air*. My life is active, active, active... *Perspiration* is my game".

SALTY likes to have visitors, so HE built a MANSION, a SALTY one. SALTY'S MANSION has a roof made of Macaroni and Cheese, walls of pOtatO chips, and floors of Crispy Corn. The ceiling is made of French fries and the WINdOwS of thinly sliced CRISPY baCON. All the dOOrs are made of pizzA, and all the knobs of fried mozzarella sticks. The furniture is built with Pretzels and Hot Dogs.

The Buds love SALTY'S MANSION. On each *trip* they take, they **can't wait** to visit HIM. As soon as they enter, they take a mouthFUL of the Macaroni and Cheese roof and a **huge bite** of the pOtatO chip walls. Then, they *gobble* on the Crispy Corn floors, they **Crunch** a GIANT serving of the French Fries ceiling and a large portion of the thinly sliced CRISPy baCON wINdOwS. To follow, they mUnch a GIGANTIC taste of the pizzq dOOrs, and they *Wolf down* all of the fried MOZZarella Sticks knobs. To finish, they *swallow*, one by one, all the *Pretzels* and *Hot Dog furniture*.

The more the Bugs bite, gobble, Crunch, Wolf down and swallow SALTY'S MANSION the more they are thirsty and blOated. First, their ankles puff-up. Then, their Legs puff-up. Lastly, their entire bodies start to swell. They get BIGGER, BIGGER, and BIGGER. They become puffier, puffier, and puffier.

They are so **puffy**, they have to hold on to each other

to avoid

flying away like ballOOns.

SALTY looks at the Buds and THINKS:

"Like all the other *field trips*, the Buds couldn't *manage* themselves. They always **bite**, *gobble*, **C**runch, *Wolf down* and *swallow* too much of my SALTY MANSION".

Then, SALTY talks to the Buds:

"Hey yo, Buds......Why don't you learn? Mine is a SALTY MANSION I understand your Excitement, pals, but just take a *nibble*, grab ONE slice. Why do you never learn, guys? *Balance* is the *key*. Not **too much**, not too little".

While SALTY is speaking, the Buds slowly manage to roll up,

Wipe off some pizza crumbs and fit their puffy

bodies on the BUS.

On their BUS, the Buds try to sing and dance. They know

how Fun it is to visit the TEENY TINY TOWN OF TASTE, but they are too thirsty

and too blOated. They can only whisper their usual song.

"We are Buds and we like to have Fun. We take trips to the

state of TONGUE.

We STOP here and we STOP there, the TOWN OF TASTE is like a

Fair".

TIRED, Weary, exhausted, drained, Sleepy, drowsy, and now even thirsty and blOated, the Bugs MUST STOP somewhere. So, they decide to STOP at the nearby home of Sour.

Sour is a Sharp guy, the Sharpest resident of the TEENY TINY TOWN OF TASTE. He is So Sharp that He rarely has visitors. He often spends time alone.

"Few Buds ask for me. Few Buds want me. Few Buds comes this way. I know why. At first, I'm too intense. But I'm a SURFER, and I'm passionate about SURFING. There is a special Wave that I like to SURF. My Wave is called Saliva. SURFING Saliva is cool! Saliva and I keep the TEENY TINY TOWN OF TASTE clean".

Sour would like to have more visitors, so He built a very nice BEACH HUT, a Sour one. Sour's BEACH HUT has a ROOF made of LEMONS, walls of Oranges and floor of lime. The Porch is built with juicy grapefruits and the front dOOr with green tomatoes. The four Windows are made of plain Greek Yogurt and the few pieces of Furniture are built with Cranberries and kiwi.

The Buds still don't know if they like Sour's BEACH HUT. This is one of their RARE VISITS. When they enter, they look around and look around.

After a few minutes, they take a small bite of the LEMON ROOF, a little nibble of the Orange walls and a tiny taste of the Lime floor. Then, they take just a savor of the juicy Grapefruit Porch, and they slurp a tiny scoop of the plain Greek Yogurt Windows. Finally, they take a small HELPING of the Cranberries and kiwi Furniture.

The more the Buds bite, *nibble*, **taste**, Savor and Slurp Sour's BEACH HUT, the more they Like it. After a few minutes, the Buds are no longer thirsty, and their *digestion* improves within seconds. Their bodies *slowly* Deflate, and they don't look like ballOOns any longer. They feel *Light* and Vigorous.

The Buds l∞k at each other SURPRISED. They have learned that Sour's BEACH HUT is delicious and refreshing.

Now, the Buds lOve Sour's BEACH HUT!

Sour looks at the Buds Warmly and thinks:

"I'm happy to see the Buds hanging out in My BEACH HUT. It may be Sharp, but it is also tasty"!

Then, Sour talks to the Buds:

"Mine is a Sour BEACH HUT, I understand why it took you so long, BROTHERS, but now you know. It is good to try something new sometimes, it is fine to give someone a chance. Quantity is the secret. Not **too large**, not too little. MAHALO, brothers. Thank you for coming. See you next time. ALOHA".

While Sour is speaking, the Buds quickly get up, clean off some LeMON juice and Jump on their BUS. Their field trip must continue. After their great experience at Sour's BEACH HUT, they want to visit the ENTIRe TEENY TINY TOWN OF TASTE!

This time, on the BUS, the Buds sing Beautifully and dANCe Gracefully.

"We are Buds and we like to have Fun. We take trips to the STATE of TONGUE. We STOP here and we STOP there, the TOWN OF TASTE is like a Fair".

Travelling and Beautifully singing, singing and Gracefully dancing, the Buds decide to STOP, for the very first time, at the home of Bitter.

Bitter is a STRONG guy, the STRONGEST resident of the TEENY TINY TOWN OF TASTE. He is SO STRONG that He scares visitors away.

"No Buds ever ask for me. No Buds ever want me. No Buds ever come this way. I know why. At first, I'm TOO STRONG, but I'm a Yoga Teacher and that is why I'm STRONG. I always Meditate and Stretch, Stretch and Meditate. I'm so Wise, I can recognize if a DANGER is near. If Sour keeps the TEENY TINY TOWN OF TASTE Clean, I keep it SAFE".

Bitter would like to have visitors, so he built a lovely eco-friendly Tree house. Bitter's eco-friendly Tree house has solar panels made of Spinach, double walls of Broccoli, and High efficiency lighting of Green Cabbage. The double glazed windows are made from Kale, and the insulation from Radish. All the WIND TURBINES are built with DARK CHOCOLATE, the Water conservation system with artIchokes, and the RECYCLING SYSTEM with ARUGULA.

The Bugs have never been to Bitter's eco-friendly Tree house, this is their very first visit. As soon as they enter, they look around and look around. Then, they look around some more.

After a few minutes, they take a small bite of the Spinach solar panels, a little nibble of the Broccoli double walls, and a tiny taste of the Green Cabbage High efficiency lighting. Then, they take a small morsel of the Kale double glazed windows, a little Savor of the Radish insulation, and a minute scoop of the DARK CHOCOLATE WIND TURBINES. Finally, they eat a modest HELPING of the artichokes Water conservation system, and they take a rapid lick of the ARUGULA RECYCLING SYSTEM.

The more the Bugs bite, nibble, taste, scoop and lick Bitter's eco-friendly Tree house, the more they Like it. After a few minutes, the Bugs feel STRONG, and their mood improves within seconds. They no longer need to visit Sweetie's Big Castle every day.

The Bugs look at each other surprised. They have learned that Bitter's eco-friendly Tree house is Tasty and INVIGORATING. Now, the Bugs love Bitter's eco-friendly Tree house!

Bitter's looks at the Buds tenderly and Thinks:

"I'm Happy to see the Buds finally enjoying My eco-friendly Tree house. It may be STRONG, but it is also

delicious"!

Then, Bitter talks to the Buds:

"Mine is a Bitter eco-friendly Tree house, I understand your hesitation, my dears. But now you know, it is good to BE ADVENTUROUS sometimes, it is fine to experiment. Portions are the secret. Not **too large**, not too little. Thank you for trying. See you soon. Namaste".

While Bitter is speaking, the Buds ENERGETICALLY get up, brush off some ARUGULA LEAVES and Jump on their BUS. Their field trip is finished for today but tomorrow is fun time all over again! They will go for another field trip to the TEENY TINY TOWN OF TASTE.

On the BUS, the Buds sing even more Beautifully and dANCE even more Gracefully than ever before. NOW, they know how Fun it is to visit the ENTIRE TEENY TINY TOWN OF TASTE.

NOW, they have learned how to use Moderation and Balance, they have learned how to care about Quantity and Portions.

Only NOW, they can have unforgettable fun in the

TEENY TINY TOWN OF TASTE.

"We are Buds and we like to have Fun. We take *trips* to the

STATE of TONGUE.

We STOP here and we STOP there, the TOWN OF TASTE is like a Fair.

Sweetie and SALTY give us pleasure only if we know how to

Measure.

If we need a good *digestion*, it's Sour and Bitter without a

Question".

One day, in the TEENY TINY TOWN OF TASTE, as life is carrying on as normal, the usual BUS brings a new visitor.

Sweetie, SALTY, Sour, and Bitter are surprised to see someone new.

"This is not the usual Bus! This is a new visitor"?! They all think with ALARM.

Bitter, the STRONGEST and most COURAGEOUS, moves one step closer and asks:

"WHO ARE YOU? WHERE DO YOU COME FROM? WHY ARE YOU VISITING the TEENY TINY TOWN OF TASTE"?

The new visitor responds with a Quiet but Clear voice:

"My name is mami and I come from apan".

SALTY jumps on his Skateboard, moves closer and with his Sharp attitude says:

"Umami!?!?!?! What kind of name is this? I have never heard of you"!

The new visitor Smiles:

"I know! Few people know me. Some people don't even like me.

Others love me for no reason at all, just because My name sounds Exotic and Fancy".

Sour puts his SURFBOARD under his arm and with his Sharp manners speaks his mind:

"WHAT DO YOU WANT? WE DON'T WANT NEW VISITORS HERE!

This TEENY TINY TOWN is too TINY, even for S"!

Umami Kindly Replies:

"I like the TEENY TINY TOWN OF TASTE. There is space for All of Us. It is just a matter of getting to know me, my Personality, and what I bring to the Table. Maybe you will like me".

Salty, Sour, and Bitter are all opposed:

"A MATTER OF GETTING TO KNOW YOU AND YOUR PERSONALITY?!

We don't have TIME to get to know Different People! We don't NEED what you bring to the Table! We ALREADY KNOW what we like!

We are not going to try ANYTHING Different! You CAN'T stay! This is OUR town! This TEENY TINY TOWN OF TASTE is already too TINY even for US".

But Sweetie interrupts her friends:

"Wait a second, my Sweetheart friends. I have been *thinking*, getting to know something DIffeREnT may be Fun! Take the Bugs for example. They used to come visit only SALTY'S MANSION and My **Big Castle**, until one day, they took the *time* to visit the ENTIRe TEENY TINY TOWN OF TASTE, and now they are Happier. Now, they lOve all of us! They have learned how to *use* Moderation and Balance, they have learned how to *care about* Quantity and Portions, with ALL of US".

Sweetie decides to get to know Umami better and asks:

"You talk about what you can bring to the Table... who are you and what do you like"?

Umami replies without thinking:

"I'm very Delicious! I'm very Enjoyable! I'm a Zen philosopher and I enjoy thinking. I think, I reason, I contemplate, and I reflect about how Delicious life can be".

Sweetie is touched by such an **Intelligent** statement. She l**oo**ks at her **Big Castle** and thinks:

"Now that the **Buds** have learned how to visit the ENTIRe TEENY TINY TOWN OF **TASTE**, how to *use Moderation* and *Balance*, how to *care about Quantity* and *Portions*, I don't need such a **Big Castle**...May be we could build a home for **U**mami. I'm sure we can all use some **Deliciousness** around HEre".

Sweetie turns around and speaks to the others:

"SALTY, S**o**ur, and **Bitter**, we have lived in the TEENY TINY TOWN OF **TASTE** for a *VERY LONG TIME*. We have **VERY** DIffeREnT personalities but we ALL bring something unique to this Table.

We have DifferEnT tools to help the TEENY TINY TOWN OF TASTE be a

better place, a wholesome place, a FUN place.

Umami is right, it is just a matter of getting to know something

different. Everybody can bring a new talent to our

Wonderful TOWN OF TASTE.

Why don't we let Umami stay? She seems Delicious!

Now that the Buds have learned how to visit the ENTIRe TEENY

TINY TOWN OF TASTE, how to use Moderation and Balance, how to

care about Quantity and Portions, I don't need such a Big

Castle...maybe we could build a Home for Umami".

SALTY, Sour, and Bitter look at each other. Then, they look around at their TEENY TINY TOWN OF TASTE. SALTY looks at his MANSION, Sour at his BEACH HUT, and Bitter at his eco-friendly Tree house... Sweetie's words have changed their mind.

"OKIE DOKIE".

They all say, and then they add:

"Umami can stay! For sure, we can use some Deliciousness ARound Here! We will build a Home for Umami, a Delicious one! Let's get to Work".

For days and days, Everybody worked **hard** in the TEENY TINY TOWN OF TASTE and today, Sweetie, SALTY, Sour, and Bitter are no longer the only REsidents of the TEENY TINY TOWN OF TASTE. Thanks to Umami they have learned to accept what is Different. Just like the Buds before them!

Today, Sweetie, SALTY, Sour, Bitter and Umami happily share the TEENY TINY TOWN OF TASTE.

Sweetie has a **smaller castle**, and SALTY has a LITTLE MANSION. Sour built a second floor in his BEACH HUT, Bitter expanded his *eco-friendly Tree house* and... even Umami has a lovely Tatami Room, all for Herself.

The Buds love Umami's Tatami Room. With each *trip* they take, they can't wait to visit her.

As soon as they enter, they take a small **bite** of the **Mushroom ceiling**, and a little *nibble* of the Parmigiano walls. Then, they take a small Sip from the broth and soy sauce Fountain, and a little Savor of the Ham Futon. Lastly, they *eat*, little by little, all the RIPE TOMATOES and Cabbage FURNiture.

When they **bite**, *nibble*, Sip, and Savor Umami's Tatami Room, the Buds feel full of Energy. They are ready to think, reason, LEARN, play, and have FUN visiting the ENTIRE TEENY TINY TOWN OF TASTE.

Several times a day, the Buds Jump on their BUS and go for a field trip to the ENTIRE teeny tiny town of TASTE. They always find time to visit All the REsidents. They know how much fun they can have if they use Moderation and Balance, if they care about Quantity and Portions when they visit Sweetie, SALTY, Sour, Bitter and Umami.

On their BUS, the Buds sing and dance because they know

well how fun it is to visit the ENTIRE teeny tiny town of TASTE.

"We are Buds and we like to have fun. We take *trips* to the

state of TONGUE.

We STOP here and we STOP there, the TOWN OF TASTE is like a fair.

Sweetie and SALTY give us Pleasure only if we know how to

Measure.

If we need good *digestion*, it's Sour and Bitter without a

Question.

As for Umami we were suspicious but then we learned she is

Delicious".

TASTING

Come Visit the Teeny Tiny Town of Taste is a book about *tasting*. My intent is to teach the next generation about our ability to enjoy food by understanding how to involve our senses. I believe that, by learning how to *taste* (involving sight, smell, taste and touch), children will naturally develop healthy eating habits and a moderate approach to food.

Tasting encourages slowing down to enjoy every bite. It promotes a positive interest in colors, shapes, aromas and flavors. It inspires shopping for the best ingredients available. It pushes us to take the time to cook home-made food, set a nice table and sit down to share a meal. In short, I believe tasting has the power to switch our outlook toward food from just nutrition or addiction to a passion and a pleasure.

I truly believe that the best gift for our children, grandchildren, nieces and nephews or other little friends is to help them understand their capacity to look, smell, taste and touch food with love, curiosity, appreciation and fun.

For all these reasons, I have put together a small section to briefly explain our capacity to taste. As I did for my previous children's book (*Coratina, A Little Lost Olive on a Journey of Discovery*), I will touch upon some important guidelines that can help parents or educators address some of the questions that may arise from reading this book.

Every day, *tasting panels* around the world taste all sorts of food to describe their sensory profile or guarantee their quality. I believe that every human being has the same potential as *professional tasters*, the only requirements are knowledge, awareness and practice.

When we eat, our senses have the ability to perceive certain food characteristics (for example, *colors*, *shapes*, *aromas*, *tastes*, *temperature*, *texture*, and *aftertastes*). Because these characteristics are perceived by the human senses, they are called *sensory characteristics*. Sensory characteristics could be positive (and help describe the food sensory profile), or negative (and allow quality evaluation).

As human beings, we naturally capture food sensory characteristics through our eyes, nose and mouth.[1] Once these characteristics are captured, the appropriate receptors (*ephitelium*, *nasal cavity*, *taste buds*, *thermoreceptors* and *chemoreceptors*) send a message to the brain. The brain reacts to this message in different ways. One way is by accessing our memory. In our memory, the brain finds terms to describe the message received.

Think about our memory as a *bank* that holds the appropriate terms for all sensory characteristics of different food. The brain access our *memory bank* looking for a term to describe the message received. If the brain finds that term, it is able to describe the message received. If the brain doesn't find that term, it is not able to describe the message. The brain can only find terms previously stored in our memory bank and appropriately labeled.

Let me give you an example. When our eyes capture a certain color, specific receptors send a message to the brain. Once the brain receives the message, among other reactions, it looks in our memory bank searching for a term to describe it. If the name of that color has been stored and labeled as "red", the brain is able to recognize, react and describe that color.

---

[1] We can also capture food sensory characteristics with our touch and hearing. For example, some chocolate tasters will touch the chocolate bar for a visceral sensation and will hear the sound of the chocolate bar breaking to determine freshens.

The ability to recognize, react[2] and describe a "certain color" as the "color red" helps us explain what we see to others because we all understand a codified and common vocabulary.

With this knowledge, we can express ourselves and share our opinions with others. A person or a child with limited vocabulary will be challenged throughout his or her life to describe and communicate effectively reactions, emotions and opinions about food.

The process of capturing colors (or smells and tastes) and sending messages to the brain is a natural ability. However, it needs some guidance. When we were young, someone told us that a "certain color" is "red". We went ahead and labeled that "certain color" with the label "red". For this reason, today when we see that "certain color", we can recognize it and describe it to others as the color "red". We simply read a label. Others react and recognize our statement because they have stored the same color with the same label.

The same is true for food sensory characteristics. If we have never given too much thought to tasting, and we are used to shoveling food in our mouth and chewing as fast as we can, our brain can't recognize (and therefore describe) all aromas, tastes, flavors or mouthfeel. We simply have not taken the time to label all aromas, tastes, flavors or mouthfeel. We have not tapped into our wonderful tasting abilities...yet.

If this is the case, we may need to start looking, smelling, tasting, storing and labeling more often to be able to fully take advantage of the great potentials of our senses.

If recognizing food colors or shapes is easy, generally because in our schooling system these characteristics are part of our education, the same is not true for aromas and tastes.

---

[2] Reactions, emotions or opinions of colors, shapes, smells or tastes are different because they are tied to our background.

That's why this section of the book may be helpful for parents.

Let's see together how our senses work while we eat and gain a little awareness of our amazing skill of tasting food.

A. *Sight.* Sight is the first sense to be activated during a tasting as colors and shapes contribute to the quality evaluation and profile description of our dish.

Through the visual cerebral center, our eyes capture images. Specific receptors (*ephitelium*) codify and translate these images. Once the images are translated, receptors send a message to the brain. Our brain receives this message and, if we have filled our memory bank with the appropriate terms, it will also be able to recognize, react and describe it.

When we take the time to look at a dish, we have the ability to naturally determine: *General Aspect* of the plate (how inviting the dish looks); *Presentation* of the food (aesthetic appearance of food and decorations); *Freshness* of the ingredients (colors and shapes should be typical of the ingredients used to prepare the dish[3]); and *Harmony* of the dish (the perfect layout and fusion of all colors and shapes).

All of these characteristics are very important to determine food quality and describe a dish profile.

B. *Smell.* The sense of smell is extremely sharp, and it can instinctively capture dozens of aromas. When we smell, aromas dissolve in the mucus and reach a tissue located at the top of the nasal cavity, behind the eyes (*olfactory epithelium*). Inside this tissue, specific receptors (*olfactory receptors*) capture the aromas and send a message to the brain. Our brain is

---

[3] Even in complex preparation it is still important to be able to perceive original colors.

able to recognize this message and react to it only if we have already experienced and stored these aromas in our memory bank. Once the reaction is there, it can be translated into words and described.

Just as we train our children to label a "certain color" as the "color red" or a "certain shape" as the "circle", we can help them label a "certain smell" as "basil". If we have never helped them label aromas and flavors, how can their brain react to a message sent by their receptors? Their brain will receive a message and, by looking in an empty memory bank, it will not be able to describe that message.

When we take the time to smell a dish (or better, when we take the time to let the aromas of the dish rise to our nose), we have the ability to naturally determine: *Freshness* (the aromas should be typical of the ingredients used to prepare that dish); *Harmony* (the perfect fusion of aromas of all ingredients); and *Quality* (the quality of aromas shows fresh and well prepared ingredients).

Besides smelling, there is another way for us to capture aromas. Since the nose and mouth share a passage (*retro-nasal passage*), while food is in our mouth, more receptors are able to (re)capture aromas and send a second message to the brain. Follow me as I explain this concept in more detail in the next section.

C. *Taste*. The sense of taste allows us to perceive food sensory characteristics thanks to about ten thousand taste buds located in our tongue[4], and thanks to other receptors located

---

[4] Taste buds are situated inside the papillae located all over our mouth, except for the center. Taste buds die and regenerate themselves every 1-2 weeks. In addition to sending messages to the brain, our taste buds also initiate salivation. This natural and instinctive process helps with a number of specific necessities and makes it easier to keep our mouth fresh and clean.

on the roof of the mouth, in the back of the throat, and on the gums.

Taste buds are responsible for detecting five *basic tastes*: *sweet*, *salty*, *sour*, *bitter* and *umami*. Other receptors are responsible for detecting *temperature* (food warmth profile), *texture* (food tactile profile), and *aftertastes* (food profile left over after swallowing).

In addition, as mentioned above, we are able to (re)detect aromas thanks to more receptors located on the very back of the mouth, exactly where the nose meets the tongue. Because of their position, these receptors are called *retro-nasal receptors*.

This natural ability of the human body to (re)detect aromas in the mouth is really worth understanding and passing on to the next generation. Besides perceiving aromas when we smell, thanks to a couple of interesting natural phenomenon, we perceive aromas also while we eat. First, when we chew with a closed mouth, our movement pushes puffs of air up toward the nose. Second, when we swallow with a closed mouth we exhale through the nose. Because nose and mouth share a passage (*retro-nasal passage*), when we chew and when we swallow, residual aromas in our mouth enter in contact with receptors (*retro-nasal receptors*) capable of (re)detecting aromas. These receptors (re)capture aromas and send a second message to the brain.

Aromas perceived when we smell are called *forward aromas*. Aromas perceived while we eat are called *retro-nasal aromas*.

Taste buds and all other receptors in our mouth capture *basic tastes*, *retro-nasal aromas*, *temperature*, *texture*, and *aftertastes* of different food. Then, they send a message to the brain. The brain recognizes this message and reacts to it. As briefly mentioned with the examples of the color red and the circle, the brain can recognize and react only to what it has already experienced, labeled and stored in a memory bank. Simply because we told our children that a "certain color" is called "red" and "certain shape" is called "circle", they are now able to recognize them, react to them, and describe them in a way that others will understand.

The same is true for food's *basic tastes*, *retro-nasal aromas*, *temperature*, *texture*, and *aftertastes*. If we never took the time to explain that a specific intense sensation is called "salty" or that a food with a velvety mouthfeel sensation is called "smooth", how can they know?

The problem is that as adults we sometimes do not know or undervalue how important recognizing these food characteristics can be for our awareness and wellbeing. The simple act of capturing, recognizing and describing colors, shapes, aromas and tastes has a natural ability to keep our brain vibrant and alert. Not to mention the rewarding feeling of being able to describe and communicate effectively reactions, emotions and opinions about food.

Understanding the wonder of our senses and learning the mechanisms and terminology connected to *tasting* is exciting and can potentially keep us healthy. Sharing this knowledge with our children means giving them a precious gift.

When we take the time to taste our food, we have the ability to naturally determine: *basic tastes* (sweet, sour, salty, bitter and umami); *retro-nasal aromas* (food sensory characteristics similar to aromas but perceived while food is in our mouth); *thermal sensations* (food temperature); *tactile sensations* (food texture); and *aftertastes* (food gustatory profile perceived after swallowing). All of these characteristics are very important to determine food quality and describe a dish profile. All of these characteristics are very important to be able to enjoy food consciously, with love, curiosity, appreciation and fun.

Follow me in the next few pages where I will describe these terms in more detail[5].

[5] For the nature of this book, some sensory concepts are simplified. For more information, consult: Lawless, Harry. Heymann, Hildegarde. *Sensory Evaluation of Food: Principles and Practices* (Boca Raton: CRC Press, 2006). Or Stone, Herbert. Bleibaum, Rebecca. Thoma, Heather. *Sensory Evaluation Practices* (San Diego: Academic Press, 2012).

RESIDENTS OF THE TOWN OF TASTE

In any tasting, our mouth is capable of perceiving five *basic tastes*: sweet, salty, sour, bitter and umami. Sweet, SALTY, Sour, Bitter and Umami are also the main characters of my book.

Sweet: This basic taste is perceived as a pleasant sensation triggered by a sweet tendency food (for example, potatoes or pasta); or by sugar added during any stage of a recipe (for example, cakes or cookies).

For a natural process, the more sweet food we eat, the more we desire it and the less we can taste it. When we eat sweet food, our taste buds send a nerve impulse to the brain. The brain perceives the message and sends a signal to eat more.

However, the more we eat sweet food the more our taste buds will get used to that level of sweetness, and they will need more in order to perceive it. For this reason, ingesting less sweet food and incorporating more of the other basic tastes is very important to rebalance this mechanism and have a more discerning approach to tasting.

SALTY: This basic taste is perceived as a intense and pungent sensation capable of inducing salivation[6] and enhancing other flavors.

A salty taste is primarily triggered by the presence of salt or salted ingredients added during any stage of a recipe. In fact, only a few foods are salty by nature (for example, oysters and shellfish). Instead, there are quite a few salted ingredients considering that salt is used for preserving or aging (for example, *Prosciutto* or *Parmigiano*).

Although people's perception of this basic taste varies drastically, salt is like sugar, the less we use it the more we improve our ability to detect it.

Sour: This basic taste is considered the opposite of sweet[7], and it is perceived as a tart and sharp sensation capable of inducing salivation.

A sour taste is triggered by food with a sour composition (for example, oranges, lemons, limes and tomatoes); or by fermented products (for example, yogurt or vinegar).

Bitter: This basic taste is the most sensitive of all for a couple of interesting reasons. First, it is perceived as unpleasant because, as a survival tool against toxic elements (generally bitter), humans are not programmed to like it. Second, considering that this taste is persistent and it lingers after swallowing, it can potentially make an unpleasant experience last longer.

---

[6] Salivation generally provides a nice cleansing effect to the mouth.

[7] However, many *sour tendency foods* also contain sweet characteristics (for example, red currant).

A bitter taste is triggered by food with a bitter composition (for example, spinach, kale, green cabbage, and eggplant; or tea and coffee with no cream, milk and sugar; or dark chocolate).[8]

Umami: Over the years, experts have added to the four basic tastes a fifth one: *Umami*. Perceived by our taste buds, umami is a Japanese term defined around 1909 by Professor Kikunae Ikeda. Umami is difficult to translate into English. It suggests a *pleasant savory taste*, or, more generally, something *delicious*.

This taste is triggered by the presence of glutamate, most notable in broth, fish, shellfish, cured meats, mushrooms, some vegetables (for example, ripe tomatoes), and fermented or aged products (for example, soy sauce and aged cheeses)[9].

---

[8] I would like to share with you my reason for representing bitter as a yoga teacher in my book. Nowadays, in the era of violent videogames, I often see strength described only as a physical power. If someone is strong, that someone must have muscles. This may be the wrong message to give our children. Strength can be a quality of the mind. It can be the power of kindness (even in hard times), perseverance, tenacity and determination. I feel that in a lifetime, all these attributes are much more important and can provide far more strength than muscles.

[9] A human's first encounter with this taste is with breast milk.

OTHER FOOD CHARACTERISTICS

The characteristics described in the previous pages are *basic tastes*. Our mouth can also naturally perceive *retro-nasal aromas* (food sensory characteristics similar to aromas but perceived while food is in our mouth); *thermal sensations* (food temperature); *tactile sensations* (food texture)[10]; and *aftertastes* (food gustatory profile perceived after swallowing).

Here are just a few more terms to describe our food. Try to pass these terms along to your children. You will be surprised how much more effectively they can express their opinions about food and how they will be more interested in the quality of what they eat.

AROMATIC: A dish can be described as *Aromatic* if it releases a wide set of aromas. Initially, the aromatic qualities of a dish are perceived by our nose as aromas (*forward aromas*) and only later by our mouth thanks to the retro-nasal passage (*retro-nasal aromas*).

An aromatic quality is primarily triggered by the presence of aromatic components added during any stage of a recipe (for example, herbs such as oregano, sage, basil or rosemary; spices such as cinnamon or nutmeg; and bulbs such as garlic). In fact, only a few foods are aromatic by nature (for example, mushrooms and shellfish).

This attribute could also be triggered by aging techniques (for example, *Pecorino* cheese is aromatic because it ages); or by some techniques that include aromatic components (for example, *Gorgonzola* cheese is aromatic because it contains strings of mold).

---

[10] *Thermal and tactile sensations* are called *mouthfeel*.

SMOOTH: A dish can be described as *Smooth* if it has a rich or velvety feel. This attribute is considered a *tactile sensation* because it is perceived by our mouth as a "touch". Just as sandpaper feels rough and velvet feels smooth on our fingertips, food also has a "touch" (a *tactile sensation* or more specifically a *mouthfeel sensation* simply because it is a feeling perceived by our mouth). We are able to perceive a food's tactile sensation thanks to receptors, located all over our mouth, that work exactly like those on our fingertips. A smooth sensation simply describes a rich *mouthfeel* (a velvety touch).

A smooth sensation is triggered by the presence of oil and fat (both animal and vegetable) added at any stage of a recipe, or by mayonnaise and olive oil used as a dressing.

SPICY: A dish can be described as *Spicy* if it offers a pungent or hot sensation. This attribute is considered a *thermal sensation* for an interesting reason. Spicy food stimulates specific fibers in our mouth (*somatosensory fibers*). These fibers send a message to the brain through specific receptors (*thermoreceptors* and *chemoreceptors*). Because these fibers and receptors are tied to our nervous system, the brain perceives the message as a burning sensation.[11]

A spicy sensation (or *pungency*) is triggered in different degrees by some vegetables (for example, chili peppers); or some spices (for example, black pepper, ginger and horseradish).

SUCCULENT: A dish can be described as *Succulent* if it has a moist or juicy mouthfeel. This attribute is also a *tactile sensation* and it is perceived inside the entire oral cavity as a juicy and moist *mouthfeel sensation*.

---

[11] It is important to remember that too much pungency can desensitize our taste buds and lower our ability to taste.

A succulent sensation is triggered in different degrees by the biological composition of an ingredient (for example, a juicy apple); or by certain liquids added during any stage of the recipe (for example, broth or wine).

MEET ORIETTA

Orietta was born and raised in Rome, Italy. She moved to Northern California in 2008, conveniently close the the best wine and olive oil production.

Orietta is particularly passionate about food, wine and olive oil. She focuses on sensory training and advocates approaching food as a professional taster. She believes that by applying to our daily life the awareness tasters experience during their tastings we could improve our relationship with food. By learning how to slow down and take the time to admire shapes and colors, appreciate aromas, anticipate and desire the magic of "every single bite" we could enjoy food and be naturally healthy. During her tastings and cooking classes, she inspires to look for quality rather than quantity, take the time to enjoy food in terms of pleasure and consider food and wine as an overall leisure experience to be shared with friends and family.

Orietta graduated *Summa Cum Laude* in *Film Studies* and has a Masters *Summa Cum Laude* in *Editorial and Journalism*. She holds a diploma of *Sommelier* from the *Associazione Italiana Sommeliers* and a Certificate of *Olive Oil Taster (IOC/EU)*.

Orietta is the owner of ORIETTA LLC, a company that offers *Gourmet Tastings-Cooking Classes-Consumer Education* for adults and children. She is a member of the *California Olive Oil Council Taste Panel*, the *Applied Sensory Olive Oil Taste Panel* and the *Mars Chocolate-UC Davis Chocolate Panel*.

Orietta tastes honey for the *Honey and Pollination Center* at the *Mondavi Institute for Food and Wine*, and she is the Delegate in the greater Sacramento area for the *Accademia Italiana della Cucina* (*Italian Academy of Cuisine*). She is a member of the *Associazione Italiana Giornalisti* (Italian Journalist Association) and of the *Actors Guild* in Italy.

Orietta was also a member of the former *UC Davis Olive Oil Taste Panel*. She is an international judge for wine and olive oil competitions around the world and the author of *A Guide to Olive Oil and Olive Oil Tasting* and two children's books about olive oil and tasting (*Coratina* and *Come Visit the Teeny Tine Town of Taste*).

Orietta created, produced, and hosted several TV shows in Italy and in America. She is especially proud of *Di.Vino*, a food and wine show inside the *KRON 4* San Francisco/Bay Area morning news. Orietta is a regular guest on local and national TV as a food and wine expert and she is working on her fifth book.

ORIETTA.NET

MEET NATHALIE

Nathalie Fabri was born to Belgian parents who traveled extensively around the world, and who collected many works of art. Her early memories of wanting to be an artist stemmed from observing the colors in these paintings.

Nathalie is a professional artist specializing in urban landscapes and loves to use her skills to work on children's book illustrations. She is the author and illustrator of *The Goats Were Everywhere*, and she is the illustrator of *Coratina, A Little Lost Olive On a Journey of Discovery*. Nathalie has also created and published a children's magazine called *Broccoli Blue*.

When she is not creating art, Nathalie works as a French teacher and Art teacher for children. Nathalie lives with her partner and young son in San Francisco.

FABRIKATIONS.COM

THANK YOU

My dearest thanks and love, today and forever, go to my family. Thanks to illustrator and friend Nathalie Fabri. We are at our second book together, and I hope we will continue for many more to come. All I can say in this limited space is that her illustrations give reality to my imagination. She is always able to create the characters as I imagine them while I write. Actually, better! All of her artistic work is inspirational.

A special thanks to Katie Gibbs, "my editor" as I call her, because she is so nice to read and read again what I write. Thanks also to Tania Fowler, the first person to read this book and encourage me to publish it.

Thanks to the *Robert Mondavi Institute for Food and Wine Science* and particularly the *Olive Oil Center* and the *Olive Oil Taste Panel*. Thanks to the *Mars-UC Davis Chocolate Taste Panel*. Thanks to the *California Olive Oil Council* and particularly Patricia Darragh, Nancy Ash and Arden Kremer. Thanks to the *Associazione Italiana Sommelier*, and to the *Accademia Italiana della Cucina*, particularly the President Giovanni Ballarini, the General Secretary Paolo Petroni, and all the members of the Sacramento Delegation.

Thanks to the *Italian Cultural Society* in Sacramento, particularly Patrizia and Bill Cerruti; the *Italian Cultural Center* in Los Angeles; the *Italy-America Chamber of Commerce*.

RESOURCES

Lawless, Harry. Heymann, Hildegarde. *Sensory Evaluation of Food: Principles and Practices* (Boca Raton: CRC Press, 2006).

Stone, Herbert. Bleibaum, Rebecca. Thoma, Heather. *Sensory Evaluation Practices* (San Diego: Academic Press, 2012).

Pollan, Michael. *Omnivore's Dilemma* (New York: Penguin Books, 2006).

Pollan, Michael. *In Defense of Food* (New York: The Penguin Press, 2008).

Pollan, Michael. *Food Rules. An Eater's Manual* (New York: Penguin Books, 2009).

Nestle, Marion. *What to Eat* (New York: North Point Press, 2006).

Planck, Nina. *Real food: What to Eat and Why* (New York: Bloomsbury, 2006).

Petrini, Carlo. *Slow Food Nation* (New York: Rizzoli Ex Libris, 2007).

Chartier, François. *Taste Buds and Molecules: The Art and Science of Food, Wine and Flavor* (Hoboken, NJ: Wiley, 2010).

Korsmeyer, Carolyn. *Making Sense of Taste. Food and Philosophy* (New York: Cornell University Press, 1999).

Cross Giblin, James. *From Hand to Mouth* (New York: Thomas Y. Crowell, 1987).

Tannahill, Reay. *Food in History* (New York: Three River Press, 1988).

Lamensky, Sarah R.; Hause, Alan M.; Martel Priscilla A.. *On Cooking. A Textbook of Culinary Fundamentals* (Upper Saddle River, New Jersey: Prentice Hall, 2010).

Rubash, Joyce. *The Master Dictionary of Food and Wine* (Hoboken, NJ: Wiley, 1996).

Tyler Herbst, Sharon. *Food Lover's Companion: Comprehensive Definitions of over 3000 Food, Wine and Culinary Terms* (Hauppauge, NY: Barrons Education Series, 1990).

Dornenburg, Andrew; Page, Karen. *The Flavor Bible* (New York: Little Brown and Company, 2008).

Made in the USA
Charleston, SC
15 November 2016